Nicky and the Fantastic Birthday Gift

Valeri Gorbachev

North-South Books · New York · London

To Julie Amper and Marc Cheshire

Published in the United States by North-South Books Inc., New York.
Published simultaneously in Great Britain, Canada, Australia, and
New Zealand in 2000 by Nord-Süd Verlag AG, Gossau Zürich, Switzerland.
Library of Congress Cataloging-in-Publication Data is available.
A CIP catalogue record for this book is available from The British Library.
The art for this book was prepared with pen-and-ink and watercolor.
Designed by Marc Cheshire
ISBN 0-7358-1378-7 (trade binding) 10 9 8 7 6 5 4 3 2 1
ISBN 0-7358-1379-5 (library binding) 10 9 8 7 6 5 4 3 2 1
Printed in Belgium
For more information about our books, and the authors and artists
who create them, visit our web site: www.northsouth.com

It was Mother Rabbit's birthday.
Nathan, Nora, Nelly, and Ned were all hard
at work making birthday presents for her.
But not Nicky. He was outside playing.

"Hey, Nicky," the others called, "aren't you going to make a present for Mother?"
"Of course I am," said Nicky. "But I'm trying to think of something really special."

"Why don't you draw a carrot like mine?"
said Nora. "Or a tree like Ned's, or a sun like
Nathan's, or a flower like Nelly's?"

"No," said Nicky. "I'm going to draw something fantastic."

"Okay," said Nora. "But you'd better hurry up. It's time to give Mother her presents."

"Happy Birthday, Mother!" cried Nathan, Nora,
Ned, and Nelly. "Look what we made for you!"
    "Oh, thank you, my dears," said Mother.
"How nice. Now we can have a real art exhibition."

"They look wonderful," said Mother, admiring the pictures. "You did a fine job, all of you—but where is Nicky's picture? And where is *Nicky*?"

"I'm in the kitchen," Nicky called. "My picture
is so fantastic, it took a long time to draw."
"It's very interesting," said Mother, looking over
Nicky's shoulder. "What is it exactly?"

"Well," said Nicky, "it's our house, and the forest, and the sea, and all of us walking through the forest to the sea, and we're having a really good time."

"Oh, of course," said Mother.

"But that's not all!" said Nicky. "See, here we are on a big green ship, sailing across the sea, and there are seagulls flying around, and dolphins leaping, and we're having a really good time."

"Oh, my!" said Mother.

Happy Birthday, Mother!

"There's more!" said Nicky.
"Here we are sailing to a beautiful island and hundreds of people are coming out to welcome us with flowers, and a band is playing music, and we're having a really good time."

"Oh, yes. Now I see," said Mother.

"It gets even better!" said Nicky. "See, we're all at this big party, with lanterns and balloons and party hats and lots of dancing and singing . . . and . . . and . . .

and a gigantic cake with a big carrot in the middle and lots of cabbage leaves around the cake and it's the most beautiful cake ever and delicious too, and we're having a really good time—because it's your birthday, Mother."

"Here," said Nicky, handing Mother the picture.
"Happy birthday!"

"It's truly fantastic, Nicky," said Mother. "Thank you very much."
She took Nicky's picture and put it with the others—right in the middle.

"Now it's time for some birthday cake,"
said Mother. "And some singing and dancing,
and we'll all have a really good time. . . ."

And that's just what they did!

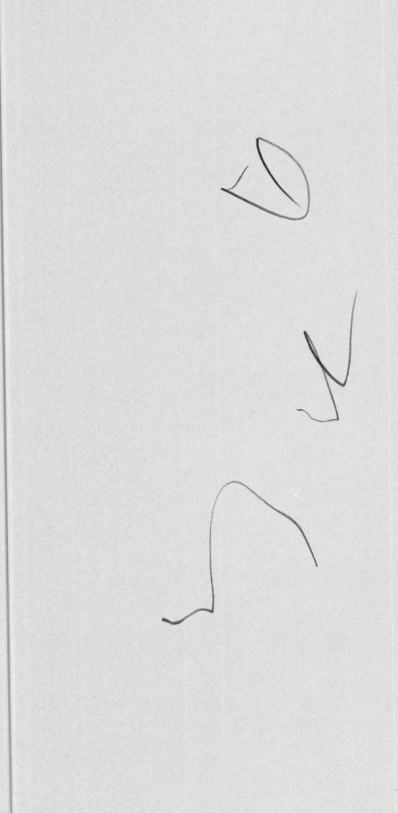